THE ENTERTAINER

PLEASE
DO NOT
FEED

KEEPER

Emma
Dodd

little bee books

An imprint of Bonnier Publishing Group

853 Broadway, New York, New York 10003

Copyright © 2014 by Emma Dodd.

This little bee books edition, 2015.

LITTLE BEE BOOKS is a trademark
of Bonnier Publishing Group,
and associated colophon is a trademark
of Bonnier Publishing Group.

Manufactured in China 0115008

First Edition 2 4 6 8 10 9 7 5 3 1

Library of Congress Control Number: 2014957618

ISBN 978-1-4998-0078-4

www.littlebeebooks.com

www.bonnierpublishing.com

Ding dong, ding dong!
Hip, hip, hooray!

There's someone
special here today. . . .

Make some room;
let him get past.

The Entertainer's
here at last!

"Come in, come in," said Billy's mom. "Tea?" Dad asked. "Please, do have some."

"Your costume looks so realistic!" The Entertainer grabbed a biscuit.

We must point out it's rather rude
to burp when someone gives you food.
I'm sure you know it's never right
to do a thing so impolite.

He drank the tea in one big slurp,
and thanked his hosts by saying,

"BURP!"

Mom looked quite shocked and said to Dad,
"His manners really are quite bad!"

The children chased him through the door
where gifts were thrown across the floor.

(Among them, Billy's gift from Mom.) He stepped....

he slipped...

he whirled...

he **spun.**

"Wow!" they cried.
"This guy is fast!"

Then
CRASH!

his journey stopped at last.

It's always best, you know, I'm sure,
to pick your toys up from the floor.
The consequences, you'll agree,
of messiness are not pain-free.

The children clapped.
The children laughed.
"He's hilarious!" they gasped.

"Hilarious?" repeated Mom.
She thought, *I wish he'd never come!*

The Entertainer grabbed a jug
and drank the water,
glug,
glug, glug.

Next, he took the flower bunch —
and chewed the stems up,
crunch,
crunch,
crunch.

And then the Entertainer found
a bowl of fruit. Mom looked and frowned.

Into his mouth, each piece he threw,
as Billy cried, "He juggles too!"

Down they went in one big bite.

"Bravo!"

the kids cried in delight.

"This guy is great!" they said to Mom.
"We're really, really glad he's come."

We advise you do not test
this hazardous way to digest.
Chewing helps release the flavor
and does your poor gut a favor.

When he'd finished
juggling fruit,
the children asked
to try on his suit.

They tugged and yanked
and poked and ripped,
but couldn't find
where it unzipped.

He stopped the kids
with big, brown paws
(attached to which
were long, sharp claws),

and reached out for a red balloon,
when— POP!

POP!

The Entertainer turned and fled—
and next door found the birthday spread!

He licked his lips, his tummy rumbled.
Over to the feast he stumbled.

Never, ever help yourselves
to laid out feasts, or food on shelves.
It is polite, I'm sure you've heard,
to wait until it has been served.

The children found him in a heap,
snoring loudly, fast asleep.

"The food!" Billy's mom cried from the hall.
"The Entertainer ate it all!"

The children laughed. "That was a treat!
But now it's time for US to eat!"

Mom dashed to the refrigerator.
"I'm glad I saved the cake for later!"

They ate the cake.
It tasted splendid!
Then the birthday
party ended.

All the guests
enjoyed the show,
but now it was time
for them to go.

Billy said, "I'm so impressed.
That Entertainer was the best!"

He added, "Mom, can I be clear?
I'd like the same one every year."

Just then, the doorbell rang,

ding dong!

A man stood with a bear-suit on.

He said, "I'm sorry I'm so late—
I went to Number 28!"